P9-DHJ-245

Best Mates

My name is

\---

I celebrated World Book Day 2015 with this
brilliant gift from my local Bookseller and
HarperCollins Children's Books

Also by Michael Morpurgo:

A Medal for Leroy

Little Manfred

An Elephant in the Garden

Shadow

Kaspar – Prince of Cats

Running Wild

The Amazing Story of Adolphus Tips

Private Peaceful

Alone on a Wide, Wide Sea

Born to Run

Sparrow

Outlaw

Pinocchio

Listen to the Moon

michael morpurgo

Best Mates

Six Favourite Stories

HarperCollins *Children's Books*

This collection first published in Great Britain by
HarperCollins *Children's Books* in 2015
HarperCollins *Children's Books* is a division of HarperCollins*Publishers* Ltd,
1 London Bridge Street, London, SE1 9GF

The HarperCollins website address is: www.harpercollins.co.uk

1

Snug, text copyright © Michael Morpurgo 1974, first published in the collection
It Never Rained in 1974 by Macmillan
The Silver Swan, text copyright © Michael Morpurgo 2000, first published in 2000
by Doubleday, a division of Penguin Random House
It's A Dog's Life, text copyright © Michael Morpurgo 2001, first published in 2001
by Egmont UK limited
Didn't We Have A Lovely Time? text copyright © Michael Morpurgo 2010,
first published in 2010 in *Country Life*
Dolphin Boy, text copyright © Michael Morpurgo, first published in 2004
by Anderson Press Ltd
This Morning I Met A Whale, text copyright © Michael Morpurgo 2008,
first published in 2008 by Walker Books Ltd
Extract from *Hero*, text copyright © Sarah Lean 2014

ISBN 978-0-00-811474-9

Printed and bound in England by Clays Ltd, St Ives plc

Contents

Snug 7

The Silver Swan 18

It's a Dog's Life 30

Didn't We Have a Lovely Time? 42

Dolphin Boy 56

This Morning I Met a Whale 65

Extract from *Hero,* by Sarah Lean 107

SNUG

Snug was Linda's cat. No one ever actually gave Linda the cat, they just grew up together. I don't really remember Linda being born, but apparently Snug turned up a few weeks earlier than she did. Dad found him wandering about, crying and mewing after a cat shoot in the barns – they shot them once in a while because they breed so fast. He found Snug crying round the calf pens. His mother must have been killed, or maybe she had run off.

Anyway, Dad picked him up and brought him home. He was so young that his eyes weren't open yet and Mum had to feed him warm milk with an eye dropper.

By the time Linda was born, Snug was a healthy kitten. Linda used to cry a lot – it's the first thing

I remember about her – come to think of it, she still howls more than she should. Snug took to curling up underneath her cot when she was indoors, and by her pram if she was sleeping outside.

I first remember noticing that Linda and Snug went together when Linda was learning to walk. She was staggering about the kitchen doing a record-breaking run from the sink to the kitchen table, all five feet of it, when Snug sidled up to her and gently nudged her off balance into the dog bowl, which was full of water. We all fell about laughing while Linda sat there howling.

He adored Linda and followed her everywhere. He'd even go for walks with her, provided she left the dog at home. Linda used to bury her face in his fur and kiss him as if he was a doll, but he loved it and stretched himself out on his back waiting for his tummy to be tickled. Then he'd purr like a lion and shoot his claws in and out in blissful happiness.

Snug grew into a huge cat. I suppose you would call him a tabby cat, grey and dusty-white merging stripes with a tinge of ginger on his soft belly. He had great pointed ears, which he flicked and twitched even when he was asleep.

He came in every evening for his food, but he never really needed it, or if he did he certainly never showed it. He didn't often get into fights, and when he did, they hardly ever left a mark – he was either a coward or a champion.

He'd come in in the morning, after a night's hunting, full of mice and moles and voles, and lie down on Linda's bed, and purr himself to sleep, waking just in time for his evening meal, which Linda served him at five o'clock.

No one ever got angry with Snug and everyone who came to the house would admire him stalking through the long grass, or sunbathing by the vegetable patch, and Linda would preen herself whenever he was mentioned.

Linda could never understand why Snug killed birds. In the early summer he used to tease to death two or three baby thrushes or blackbirds a day. Linda very nearly went off him at this time every year. Only last summer he found a robin's nest at the bottom of a hedge – he'd been attracted by the cheeps. By the time we got there, he'd scooped out three baby robins and there were several speckled eggs lying broken and scattered. Linda didn't speak to him for a week, and I had to feed him. But they made it up, they always did.

Occasionally Snug wandered off into the barns and fields looking for a friendly she-cat. This must have taken a long time, because he disappeared sometimes for twenty-four hours or so – but never longer, except once.

Mum and Dad were home and Snug was late coming in. We'd had our bath and were sitting watching telly – *Tom and Jerry*, I think it was, because we always went to bed after that. There was a yowl outside the kitchen door, more like a dog in pain than a cat. Linda disappeared into the kitchen and I followed – I'd seen the *Tom and Jerry* before anyway. Linda opened the door and Snug came in, worming his way against the doorway. His head was hanging and his tail, which he usually held up straight, was drooping. One ear was covered in blood and there was a great scratch across his face. He'd been in a fight and he was badly hurt.

Linda picked him up gently and put him in his basket. 'Get the TCP and some water… quick!' she said.

Snug lay there panting while Linda cleaned up his wounds. I supplied the cotton wool and the TCP and when Linda had finished that, the Dettol.

She must have spent an hour or more nursing that cat, and all the time I didn't say a word to her: I knew she'd cry if I talked to her.

Mum came in after a bit to wash up. She bent over the basket. "He'll be all right, dear," she said. "It's not as bad as it looks. You'll see, he'll be right as rain by the morning. Why don't you see if he'll take some warm milk?"

Linda nodded. I knew she wouldn't do it herself; she'd have to turn round. She hated showing her face when she was upset. I put the milk on the stove and Mum cleared up. Linda put the saucer down by the basket and Snug went up to it almost immediately. He drank slowly, crouched over the milk, his pink tongue shooting clean into the saucer.

What happened next, happened so suddenly that none of us had time to react. Mum bent down to put some potato peel in the bin; she lifted it and opened the door to empty it. In a flash Snug was through the door, and we just stood there, the three of us, Mum clutching her bin, me holding the saucepan and Linda, her eyes red with crying.

Linda rushed after him, calling into the night. We all tried. Even Dad came away from the telly and called. But Snug would not come.

We tried to convince Linda that he'd be all right. Dad put his arm around her and stroked her hair before we went up to bed. "If he'd been really ill, love, he wouldn't have taken any milk." He was a great dad sometimes. "He'll be back tomorrow, you'll see."

We went off to school as usual the next morning. No one even mentioned Snug at breakfast. Usually we went along the road to school to meet up with Tom, but this morning Linda wanted to go through the fields. We left the house early and went off through the farm buildings where Snug used to hunt. Linda searched round the tractor sheds and calf pens, while I clambered over the straw in the Dutch barn. It was no good: there wasn't enough time. We had to get to school.

"It'll be all right, Lin," I said. "Don't worry." It was the best I could do.

School went slowly that day. Linda was even quieter than usual: she spent play-time looking over the fence into the orchard behind the playground, and during lessons she kept looking out of the window, and I could see her getting more and more worried.

Lunch came and went, and it started to rain: by the time we were let out it was pouring down. Linda grabbed her coat and rushed out. There was still no sign of Snug at home. We searched and called until it was dark and Mum came home from work. The time for his meal passed; still no Snug.

Dad came home a little later than usual. We were in the front room, Linda and I, and we heard him talking quietly to Mum in the kitchen.

We were mucking about trying to mend my train set on the floor when Dad came in. He didn't flop down in his armchair but stood there all tall and near the ceiling, and he hadn't taken his coat off. It was dripping on the carpet.

"Lin," he said. "I'm sorry, love, but we've found Snug. He's been killed, run over. Tom's father found him down by the main road. It must have been quick, he wouldn't have felt anything. I'm sorry, love."

Linda turned away.

"Are you sure it's him?" I said. "There's lots of cats like him about."

Linda ran out of the room and upstairs and Mum went up after her.

"It's him all right – I've got him in the shed outside. I thought we'd bury him tomorrow, if Lin wants us to." Dad sat down. "It's him all right, poor old thing."

"Can I have a look at him, Dad, just to be sure?" I said. I didn't feel like crying; somehow I couldn't feel sad enough. I was interested more than upset. It was strange because I really liked that cat.

Dad took me over to the shed and switched on the light. There he was, all stretched out in a huge cereal carton. He barely covered the bottom of it. His fur was matted and soaked. There was no blood or anything; he just lay there all still and his eyes closed.

"Well?" Dad mumbled behind me. "It's him, isn't it?" It *was* him, the same gingerish tummy, and the same tabby markings. He didn't look quite so big lying in that box.

"He's so still, Dad," I said. "Why isn't he all broken up after being run over? You'd think he'd be squashed or something."

"When you carry him, he doesn't feel right, but I expect he was thrown clear on impact," Dad said. "Go on now, you'd better go and see Lin."

When I got up to my bedroom, Mum was in with Linda and I could hear a lot of crying. I hate that: I never know what to say to people when they're like that. I went and lay on my bed and tried to feel sadder than I really was. I was more sorry about Lin than old Snug. He'd had a fairly good run after all, lots of food and warmth and love. What more could a cat want? And for some reason I got to thinking of a party the mice would be holding in the Dutch barn that night to celebrate Snug's death.

I was down early in the morning before anyone else. I'd forgotten to feed the goldfish the night before. I was dropping the feed in the tank, when I heard Snug's voice outside the kitchen door. There was no mistake. It was his usual "purrrrrp... p... p" – a sort of demand for immediate entry. I wasn't hearing things either. I opened the door and in he came, snaking his way round the doorpost, as happy and contented with himself as ever.

I screamed upstairs, "He's here! He's back! Snug's back!"

Well of course they didn't take long to get down-stairs, and Linda was all weeping over him and examining him as if she couldn't believe it.

Dad came back from the shed in his slippers and dressing gown. "Lin, I'm sorry, love, but it's amazing: that cat's the spitting image of Snug.

Honest he is."

Lin wasn't even listening, and I must admit I felt quite happy myself. It was a Saturday morning, Snug had come back from the dead and I was playing football that afternoon.

Dad and I buried the other cat after breakfast. We dug a hole in the woods on the other side of the stream and wrapped him in one of Dad's old gardening jackets.

When we got back, I saw Dawnie from school in the garden with Linda. Mum met us by the gate. "It was Dawn's cat," she said. "It's been missing for a couple of days and it's just like Snug. She wants to see where you've buried it."

THE SILVER SWAN

The silver swan, who living had no note,
When death approached, unlocked her silent
throat:
Leaning her breast against the reedy shore
Thus sung her first and last, and sung no more.
Orlando Gibbons

A swan came to my loch one day, a silver swan. I was fishing for trout in the moonlight. She came flying in above me, her wings singing in the air. She circled the loch twice, and then landed, silver, silver in the moonlight.

I stood and watched her as she arranged her wings behind her and sailed out over the loch, making it entirely her own. I stayed as late as I could, quite unable to leave her.

I went down to the loch every day after that,

but not to fish for trout, simply to watch my silver swan.

In those early days I took great care not to frighten her away, keeping myself still and hidden in the shadow of the alders. But even so, she knew I was there – I was sure of it.

Within a week I would find her cruising along the lochside, waiting for me when I arrived in the early mornings. I took to bringing some bread crusts with me. She would look sideways at them at first, rather disdainfully. Then, after a while, she reached out her neck, snatched them out of the water, and made off with them in triumph.

One day I dared to dunk the bread crusts for her, dared to try to feed her by hand. She took all I offered her and came back for more. She was coming close enough now for me to be able to touch her neck. I would talk to her as I stroked her. She really listened, I know she did.

I never saw the cob arrive. He was just there swimming beside her one morning out on the loch. You could see the love between them even then. The princess of the loch had found her prince. When they drank they dipped their necks together, as one. When they flew, their wings beat together, as one.

She knew I was there, I think, still watching. But she did not come to see me again, nor to have her bread crusts. I tried to be more glad for her than sad for me, but it was hard.

As winter tried, and failed, to turn to spring, they began to make a home on the small island, way out in the middle of the loch. I could watch them now only through my binoculars. I was there every day I could be – no matter what the weather.

Things were happening. They were no longer busy just preening themselves, or feeding, or simply gliding out over the loch taking their reflections with them. Between them they were building a nest – a clumsy messy excuse for a nest it seemed to me – set on a reedy knoll near the shore of their island.

It took them several days to construct. Neither ever seemed quite satisfied with the other's work. A twig was too big, or too small, or perhaps just not in the right place. There were no arguments as such, as far as I could see. But my silver swan would rearrange things, tactfully, when her cob wasn't there. And he would do the same when she wasn't there.

Then, one bright cold morning with the ground beneath my feet hard with a late and unexpected frost, I arrived to see my silver swan enthroned at last on her nest, her cob proudly patrolling the loch close by.

I knew there were foxes about even then. I had heard their cries often enough echoing through the night. I had seen their footprints in the snow. But I had never seen one out and about, until now.

It was dusk. I was on my way back home from the loch, coming up through the woods, when I spotted a family of five cubs, their mother sitting on guard nearby. Unseen and unsmelt, I crouched down where I was and watched.

I could see at once that they were starving, some of them already too weak even to pester their mother for food. But I could see too that she had none to give – she was thin and rangy herself. I remember thinking then: *That's one family of foxes that's not likely to make it, not if the spring doesn't come soon, not if this winter goes on much longer.*

But the winter did go on that year, on and on.

I thought little more of the foxes. My mind was on other things, more important things. My silver swan and her cob shared the sitting duties and the guarding duties, never leaving the precious nest long enough for me even to catch sight of the eggs, let alone count them. But I could count the days, and I did.

As the day approached I made up my mind I would go down to the loch, no matter what, and stay there until it happened – however long that might take. But the great day dawned foggy. Out of my bedroom window, I could barely see across the farmyard.

I ran all the way down to the loch. From the lochside I could see nothing of the island, nothing of the loch, only a few feet of limpid grey water lapping at the muddy shore. I could hear the muffled *aarking* of a heron out in the fog, and the distant piping of a moorhen. But I stayed to keep watch, all that day, all the next.

I was there in the morning two days later when the fog began at last to lift and the pale sun to come through. The island was there again. I turned my binoculars at once on the nest. It was deserted. They were gone. I scanned the loch, still mist-covered in places. Not a ripple. Nothing.

Then out of nothing they appeared, my silver swan, her cob and four cygnets, coming straight towards me. As they came towards the shore they turned and sailed right past me. I swear she was showing them to me, parading them. They both swam with such easy power, the cygnets bobbing along in their wake. But I had counted wrong. There was another one, hitching a ride in amongst his mother's folded wings. A snug little swan, I thought, littler than the others perhaps. A lucky little swan.

That night the wind came in from the north and the loch froze over. It stayed frozen. I wondered how they would manage. But I need not have worried. They swam about, keeping a pool of water near the island clear of ice. They had enough to eat, enough to drink. They would be fine. And every day the cygnets were growing. It was clear now that one of them was indeed much smaller, much weaker. But he was keeping up. He was coping. All was well.

Then, silently, as I slept one night, it snowed outside. It snowed on the farm, on the trees, on the frozen loch. I took bread crusts with me the next morning, just in case, and hurried down to the loch. As I came out of the woods I saw the fox's paw prints in the snow. They were leading down towards the loch.

I was running, stumbling through the drifts, dreading all along what I might find.

The fox was stalking around the nest. My silver swan was standing her ground over her young, neck lowered in attack, her wings beating the air frantically, furiously. I shouted. I screamed. But I was too late and too far away to help.

Quick as a flash the fox darted in, had her by the wing and was dragging her away. I ran out on to the ice. I felt it crack and give suddenly beneath me. I was knee-deep in the loch then, still screaming, but the fox would not be put off. I could see the blood, red, bright red, on the snow. The five cygnets were scattering in their terror. My silver swan was still fighting. But she was losing, and there was nothing I could do.

I heard the sudden singing of wings above me. The cob! The cob flying in, diving to attack. The fox took one look upwards, released her victim, and scampered off over the ice, chased all the way by the cob.

For some moments I thought my silver swan was dead. She lay so still on the snow. But then she was on her feet and limping back to her island, one wing flapping feebly, the other trailing, covered in blood and useless. She was gathering her cygnets about her. They were all there. She was enfolding them, loving them, when the cob came flying back to her, landing awkwardly on the ice.

He stood over her all that day and would not leave her side. He knew she was dying. So, by then, did I. I had nothing but revenge and murder in my heart. Time and again, as I sat there at the lochside, I thought of taking my father's gun and going into the woods to hunt down the killer fox. But then I would think of her cubs and would know that she was only doing what a mother fox had to do.

For days I kept my cold sad vigil by the loch. The cob was sheltering the cygnets now, my silver swan sleeping nearby, her head tucked under her wing. She scarcely ever moved.

I wasn't there, but I knew the precise moment she died. I knew it because she sang it. It's quite true what they say about swans singing only when they die. I was at home. I had been sent out to fetch logs for the fire before I went up to bed. The world about me was crisp and bright under the moon. The song was clearer and sweeter than any human voice, than any birdsong, I had ever heard before. So sang my silver swan and died.

I expected to see her lying dead on the island the next morning. But she was not there. The cob was sitting still as a statue on his nest, his five cygnets around him.

I went looking for her. I picked up the trail of feathers and blood at the lochside, and followed where I knew it must lead, up through the woods. I approached silently. The fox cubs were frolicking fat and furry in the sunshine, their mother close by intent on her grooming. There was a terrible wreath of white feathers nearby, and telltale feathers too on her snout. She was trying to shake them off. How I hated her.

I ran at her. I picked up stones. I hurled them. I screamed at her. The foxes vanished into the undergrowth and left me alone in the woods. I picked up a silver feather, and cried tears of such raw grief, such fierce anger.

Spring came at long last the next day, and melted the ice. The cob and his five cygnets were safe. After that I came less and less to the loch. It wasn't quite the same without my silver swan. I went there only now and again, just to see how he was doing, how they were all doing.

At first, to my great relief, it seemed as if he was managing well enough on his own. Then one day I noticed there were only four cygnets swimming alongside him, the four bigger ones. I don't know what happened to the smaller one. He just wasn't there. Not so lucky, after all.

The cob would sometimes bring his cygnets to the lochside to see me. I would feed them when he came, but then after a while he just stopped coming.

The weeks passed and the months passed, and the cygnets grew and flew. The cob scarcely left his island now. He stayed on the very spot I had last seen my silver swan. He did not swim; he did not feed; he did not preen himself. Day by day it became clearer that he was pining for her, dying for her.

Now my vigil at the lochside was almost constant again. I had to be with him; I had to see him through. It was what my silver swan would have wanted, I thought.

So I was there when it happened. A swan flew in from nowhere one day, down on to the glassy stillness of the loch. She landed right in front of him. He walked down into the loch, settled into the water and swam out to meet her. I watched them look each other over for just a few minutes. When they drank, they dipped their necks together, as one. When they flew, their wings beat together, as one.

Five years on and they're still together. Five years on and I still have the feather from my silver swan. I take it with me wherever I go. I always will.

It's a Dog's Life

Open one eye.
Same old basket, same old kitchen.
Another day.

Ear's itching.
Have a good scratch.
Lovely.

Have a good stretch.

Here comes Lula.

"Morning, Russ," she says.
"Do you know what day it is today?"
Silly question! Course I do!
It's the day after yesterday

and the day before tomorrow.

Out I go. Smarty's barking his 'good morning' at
me from across the valley.
Good old Smarty. Best friend I've got, except
Lula of course.
I bark mine back.

I can't hang about. Got to get the cows in.

There they are.
Lula's dad likes me to
have them ready for milking
by the time he gets there.

Better watch that one with the new calf.
She's a bit skippy.
Lie down, nose in the grass.
Give her the hard eye.

There she goes, in amongst the rest.

And here comes Lula's dad singing his way down

to the dairy.

"Good dog," he says.

I wag my tail. He likes that.

He gives me another 'good dog'.

I get my milk. Lovely.

Off back up to the house.

Well, I don't want to miss my breakfast, do I?

Lula's already scoffing her bacon and eggs.

I sit down next to her

and give her my

very best begging look.

It always works.

Two bacon rinds in secret under the table,

and all her toast crusts too. Lovely.

There's good pickings

under the baby's chair this morning.

I hoover it all up. Lovely.

Lula always likes me to go with her

to the end of the lane.

She loves a bit of a cuddle, and
a lick or two before the school bus comes.

"Oh, Russ," she whispers. "A horse.
It's all I want for my birthday."
And I'm thinking, *'Scuse me, what's so great*
about a horse?
Isn't a dog good enough?

Then along comes the bus and on she gets.
"See you," she says.

Lula's dad is whistling for me.
"Where are you, you old rascal you?"

I'm coming.
I'm coming.

Back up the lane,
through the hedge,
over the gate.

"Don't just sit there, Russ.

I want those sheep in for shearing."

And all the while he keeps on
with his whistling and whooping.

I mean, does he think
I haven't done this before?
Doesn't he know
this is what I'm made for?

Hare down the hill.
Leap the stream.
Get right around behind them.

Keep low. Don't rush them. That's good.

They're all going now. The whole flock of them
are trotting along nicely.
And I'm slinking along behind, my eye on every
one of them,
my bark and my bite deep inside their heads.

"Good dog," I get. Third one today. Not bad.

I watch the shearing
from the top of the haybarn.
Good place to sleep, this.

Tigger's somewhere here.
I can smell her.

There she is, up on the rafter,
waving her tail at me.
She's teasing me. I'll show her.

Later, I'll do it later.
Sleep now. Lovely.

"Russ! Where are you, Russ?
I want these sheep out.
Now! Move yourself."

All right, all right.
Down I go, and out they go,
all in a great muddle
bleating at each other,

bopping one another.

They don't recognise each other without their
clothes on.
Not very bright, that's the trouble with sheep.

Will you look at that!
There's hundreds of crows out in my corn field.

Well, I'm not having that, am I?
After them! Show them who's boss!
Thirsty work, this.

What's this? Fox!
I can smell him.
I follow him down
through the bluebell wood to his den.
He's down there, deep down.
Can't get at him. Pity.

Need a drink.
Shake myself dry in the sun.
Time for another sleep.

Lovely.

Smarty wakes me.
I know what he's thinking.
How about
a Tigger hunt?

We find her soon enough.
We're after her.

We're catching her up.
Closer. Closer.
Right on her tail.

That's not fair.
She's found a tree.
Up she goes.
We can't climb trees, so we bark our heads off.
Ah well, you can't win them all.

"Russ, where were you, Russ?"
Lula's dad. Shouting for me again.
"Get those calves out in the field.

What's the point in keeping a dog
and barking myself?"

Nothing worse than trying to move young calves.
They're all tippy-toed and skippy.
Pretty things.
Pity they get so big and lumpy when they get
older.

There, done it. Well done, me!

Back to the end of the lane to meet Lula.
I'm a bit late. She's there already,
swinging her bag and singing.

"Happy birthday to me,
happy birthday to me.
Happy birthday, dear Lula,
happy birthday to me!"

For tea there's a big cake with candles on it,
and they're singing that song again.

Will you look at them
tucking into that cake!
And never a thought for me.

Lula's so busy unwrapping her presents
that she doesn't even notice I'm there,
not even when I put my head on her knee.
Car! Car coming up my lane, and not one I know.
I'm out of the house in a flash.

I'm not just a farm dog, you know, I'm a guard
dog too.
"Russ! Stop that barking, will you?"
That's all the thanks I get.
I'm telling you, it's a dog's life.

Looks like a horse to me.
Give him a sniff.
Yes, definitely a horse.

Lula goes mad.
She's hugging the horse
just like she hugs me, only for longer.

A lot longer.

"He's beautiful," she's saying.
"Just what I wanted."

Well, I'm not staying where I'm not wanted.
I haven't had any of that cake,
and they're not watching.

Nip back inside. Jump on a chair.
I'm a champion chomper.
Ooops.
The plate's fallen off the table.
I'm in trouble now.

They all come running in.
I look dead innocent.
Doesn't fool them though.
"You rascal, you. Out you go!"

I don't care. It was worth it.

I go and sit at the top of the hill

and tell Smarty all about it.
He barks back, "Good on you!
Who wants to be a good dog, anyway?"

Then Lula's sitting down beside me.
"I really love my horse," she says,
"but I love you more, Russ. Promise."

Give her a good lick. Make her giggle.
I like it when she giggles.
Lick her again.
Lovely.

DIDN'T WE HAVE A LOVELY TIME?

I have been teaching for over twenty years now, mostly around Hoxton, in north London. After all that time I am no longer at all sentimental about children. I don't think you could be. Twenty years at the chalk face of education gives you a big dose of reality.

I was sentimental to start with, I'm sure. I am still an idealist, though not as zealous perhaps as I used to be, but the fire's still there. You could say that I have given my life to it – I've never had children of my own. I'm headmistress at the school now and I believe more than ever we should be creating the best of all possible worlds for our children, giving every one of them the best possible chance to thrive. That's why every year for at least the past ten years I've been taking the children down to a farm in Devon, a place called Nethercott.

It takes six long hours by coach from London and there, in a large Victorian manor house with views over to distant Dartmoor, we all live together, all forty of us, teachers and children. We eat three good hot meals a day, sing songs and tell stories around the fire at night, and we sleep like logs. By day we work. And that's the joy of it, to see the children working hard and purposefully out on the farm, feeding calves, moving sheep, grooming Hebe the Haflinger horse who everyone loves, mucking out stables and sheds, collecting eggs and logs, and apples too. The children do it all, and they love it – mostly, anyway. They work alongside real farmers, get to feel like real farmers, know that everything they are doing is useful and important to the farm, that they and their work are appreciated.

Every year we come back to school and the whole place is buzzing. In the playground and in the staffroom all the different stories of our week down on the farm are told again and again. The magic moments – a calf being born, the glimpse of a fox or a deer in Bluebell Wood; the little disasters – Mandy's welly sucked off in the mud, Jemal being chased by the goose. The children write a lot about it, paint pictures of it, and I know they dream about it too, as I do.

But something so extraordinary happened on one of these visits that I too felt compelled to write it down, just as it happened, so that I should never forget it – and because I know that in years to come, as memory fades, it is going to be difficult to believe. I've always found miracles hard to believe, and this really was a kind of miracle.

The boys and girls at our school, St Francis, come from every corner of the earth, so we are quite used to children who can speak little or no English. But until Ho arrived we never had a child who didn't speak at all – he'd have been about seven when he joined us. In the three years he'd been with us he had never uttered a word. As a result he had few friends, and spent much of his time on his own. We would see him sitting by himself reading. He read and he wrote in correct and fluent English, more fluent than many of his classmates who'd been born just down the street. He excelled in maths too, but never put his hand up in class, was never able to volunteer an answer or ask a question. He just put it all down on paper, and it was usually right. None of us ever saw him smile at school, not once. His expression seemed set in stone, fixed in a permanent frown.

We had all given up trying to get him to talk. Any effort to do so had only one effect – he'd simply run off, out into the playground, or all the way home if he could. The educational psychologist, who had not got a word out of him either, told us it was best simply to let him be, and do whatever we could to encourage him, to give him confidence, but without making demands on him to speak. He wasn't sure whether Ho was choosing not to speak or whether he simply couldn't.

All we knew about him was that ever since he'd arrived in England he'd been living with his adoptive parents. In all that time he hadn't spoken to them either, not a word. We knew from them that Ho was one of the Boat People, that as the war in Vietnam was coming to an end he had managed to escape somehow. There were a lot of Boat People coming to England in those days, mostly via refugee camps in Hong Kong, which was still British then. Other than that, he was a mystery to us all.

When we arrived at the farm I asked Michael – he was the farm school manager at Nethercott, and, after all these years, an old friend – to be a little bit careful how he treated Ho, to go easy on him. Michael could be blunt with the children, pointing at them, firing direct questions in a way that demanded answers. Michael was fine about it. The truth was that everyone down there on the farm was fascinated by this silent little boy from Vietnam, mostly because they'd all heard about the suffering of the Vietnamese Boat People and this was the first time they'd ever met one of them.

Ho had an aura of stillness about him that set

him apart. Even sweeping down the parlour after milking, he would be working alone, intent on the task in hand – methodically, seriously, never satisfied until the job was done perfectly.

He particularly loved to touch the animals, I remember that. Looking wasn't enough. He showed no fear as he eased his hand under a sitting hen to find a new-laid egg. When she pecked at him he didn't mind. He just stroked her, calmed her down. Moving the cows out after milking he showed no sign of fear, as many of the other children did. He stomped about in his wellies, clapping his hands at them, driving them on as if he'd been doing it all his life. He seemed to have an easiness around animals, an affinity with the cows in particular, I noticed. I could see that he was totally immersed in this new life in the country, loving every moment of every day. The shadow that seemed to hang over him back at school was lifting; the frown had gone.

On the Sunday afternoon walk along the River Okement I felt him tugging suddenly at my arm and pointing. I looked up just in time to see the flashing brilliance of a kingfisher flying straight as an arrow down the middle of the river. He and I were the only ones to see it. He so nearly smiled then. There was a new light in his eyes that I had not seen before. He was so observant and fascinated, so confident around the animals, I began to wonder about his past – maybe he'd been a country boy back in Vietnam when he was little. I longed to ask him, particularly when he came running up to walk alongside me again. I felt his cold hand creep into mine. That had certainly never happened before. I squeezed it gently and he squeezed back. It was every bit as good as talking, I thought.

At some point during our week-long visit, Michael comes up in the evening to read a story to the children. He's a bit of a writer, as well as a performer. He likes to test his stories out on the children, and we like listening to them too. He never seems to get offended if someone nods off – and they're so tired, they often do. We have all the children washed and ready in their dressing gowns (not easy, I can tell you, when there are nearly forty of them!), hands round mugs of steaming hot chocolate, and gather them in the sitting room round the fire for Michael's story.

On this particular evening, the children were noisy and all over the place, high with excitement. They were often like that when it was windy outside, and there'd been a gale blowing all day. It was a bit like rounding up cats. We thought we'd just about managed it, and were doing a final count of heads, when I noticed that Ho was missing. Had anyone seen him? No. The teachers and I searched for him all over the house. No one could find him anywhere. Long minutes passed and still no sign of Ho. I was becoming more than a little worried. It occurred to me that someone might have upset him, causing Ho to run off, just as he had a few times back at school. Out there in the dark he could have got himself lost and frightened all too easily. He had been in his dressing gown and slippers the last time anyone saw him, that much we had established. But it was a very cold night outside. I was trying to control my panic when Michael walked in, manuscript in hand.

"I need to speak to you," he said. "It's Ho." My heart missed a beat. I followed him out of the room.

"Listen," he said, "before I read to the children, there's something I have to show you."

"What?" I asked. "What's happened? Is he all right?"

"He's fine," Michael replied. "In fact, I'd say he's happy as Larry. He's outside. Come and have a look." He put his fingers to his lips. "We need to be quiet. I don't want him to hear us."

And so it was that the two of us found ourselves, minutes later, tiptoeing through the darkness of the walled vegetable garden. It was so quiet, I remember hearing a fox barking down in the valley.

There was a light on over the stable door. Michael put his hand on my arm.

"Look," he whispered. "Listen. That's Ho, isn't it?"

Ho was standing there under the light

stroking Hebe and talking to her softly. He was talking! Ho was talking, but not in English – in Vietnamese, I supposed. I wanted so much to be able to understand what he was saying. As though he were reading my thoughts, at that very moment he switched to English, speaking without hesitation, the words flowing out of him.

"It's no good if I speak to you in Vietnamese, Hebe, is it? Because you are English. Well, I know really you are from Austria, that's what Michael told us, but everyone speaks to you in English." Ho was almost nose to nose with Hebe now. "Michael says you're twenty-five years old. What's that in human years? Fifty? Sixty? I wish you could tell me what it's like to be a horse. But you can't talk out loud, can you? You're like me. You talk inside your head. I wish you could talk to me, because then you could tell me who your mother was, who your father was, how you learnt to be a riding horse. And you can pull carts too, Michael says. And you could tell me what you dream about. You could tell me everything about your life, couldn't you?

"I'm only ten, but I've got a story I could tell you. D'you want to hear it? Your ears are twitching. I think you understand every word I'm saying, don't you? Do you know we both begin with 'H', don't we? Ho. Hebe. No one else in my school is called Ho, only me. And I like that. I like to be like no one else. The other kids have a go at me sometimes, call me Ho Ho Ho – because that's how Father Christmas talks. Not very funny, is it?

"Anyway, where I come from in Vietnam, we never had Father Christmas. I lived in a village. My mum and dad worked in the rice fields, but then the war came and there were soldiers everywhere and aeroplanes. Lots of bombs falling. So then we moved to the city, to Saigon. I hated the city. I had two little sisters. They hated the city too. No cows and no hens. The city was so crowded. But not as crowded as the boat. I wish we had never got on that boat, but Mum said it would be much safer for us to leave. On the boat there were hundreds of us, and there wasn't enough food and water. And there were storms and I thought we were all going to die. And lots of us did die too, Mum and Dad, and my two sisters. I was the only one in the family left.

"A big ship came along and picked us up one day, me and a few others. I remember someone asked me my name, and I couldn't speak. I was too sad to speak. That's why I haven't spoken to anyone since then – only in my head like I said. I talk to myself in my head all the time, like you do. They put me in a camp in Hong Kong, which was horrible. I could not sleep. I kept thinking of my family, all dead in the boat. I kept seeing them again and again. I couldn't help myself. After a while I was adopted by Aunty Joy and Uncle Max and came to London – that's a long way from here. It's all right in London, but there are no cows or hens. I like it here. I want to stay here all my life. Sometimes at home, and at school, I'm so sad that I feel like running away. But with you and all the animals I don't feel sad any more."

All the time Ho was talking I had the strangest

feeling that Hebe was not only listening to every single word he said, but that she understood his sadness, and was feeling for him, as much as we did, as we stood there listening in the darkness.

Ho hadn't finished yet. "I've got to go now, Hebe," he said. "Michael's reading us a story. But I'll come back tomorrow evening, shall I? When no one else is about. Night night. Sleep tight. Don't let the bedbugs bite." And he ran into the house then, almost tripping over the doorstep as he went.

Michael and I were so overwhelmed that for a minute we couldn't speak. We decided not to talk about it to anyone else. It would seem somehow like breaking a confidence.

For the rest of the week down on the farm Ho remained as silent and uncommunicative as before. But I noticed now that he would spend every moment he could in the stable yard with Hebe. The two had become quite inseparable. As the coach drove off on the Friday morning I sat down in the empty seat next to Ho. He was looking steadfastly, too steadfastly, out of the window. I could tell he was trying his best to hide his tears. I didn't really intend to say anything, and certainly not to ask him a question. It just popped out. I think I was trying to cheer him up.

"Well, Ho, didn't we have a lovely time?"

Ho didn't turn round.

"Yes, miss," he said, soft and clear. "I had a lovely time."

DOLPHIN BOY

Once upon a time, the little fishing village was a happy place. Not any more.

Once upon a time, the fishermen of the village used to go out fishing every day. Not any more.

Once upon a time, there were lots of fish to catch. Not any more.

Now the boats lay high and dry on the beach, their paint peeling in the sun, their sails rotting in the rain.

Jim's father was the only fisherman who still took his boat out. That was because he loved the *Sally May* like an old friend and just couldn't bear to be parted from her.

Whenever Jim wasn't at school, his father would take him along. Jim loved the *Sally May* as much as his father did in spite of her raggedy old sails. There was nothing he liked better than taking the helm, or hauling in the nets with his father.

One day, on his way home from school, Jim saw his father sitting alone on the quay, staring out at an empty bay. Jim couldn't see the *Sally May* anywhere. "Where's the *Sally May*?" he asked.

"She's up on the beach," said his father, "with all the other boats. I've caught no fish at all for a week, Jim. She needs new sails and I haven't got the money to pay for them. No fish, no money. We can't live without money. I'm sorry, Jim."

That night Jim cried himself to sleep.

After that, Jim always took the beach road to school because he liked to have a look at the *Sally May* before school began.

He was walking along the beach one morning when he saw something lying in the sand amongst the seaweed. It looked like a big log at first, but it wasn't. It was moving. It had a tail and a head. It was a dolphin!

Jim knelt in the sand beside him. The boy and

the dolphin looked into each other's eyes. Jim knew then exactly what he had to do.

"Don't worry," he said. "I'll fetch help. I'll be back soon, I promise."

He ran all the way up the hill to school as fast as he could go. Everyone was in the playground.

"You've got to come!" he cried. "There's a dolphin on the beach! We've got to get him back in the water or he'll die."

Down the hill to the beach the children ran, the teachers as well. Soon everyone in the village was there – Jim's father and his mother too.

"Fetch the *Sally May*'s sail!" cried Jim's mother. "We'll roll him on to it."

When they had fetched the sail, Jim crouched down beside the dolphin's head, stroking him and comforting him. "Don't worry," he whispered. "We'll soon have you back in the sea."

They spread out the sail and rolled him on to it very gently. Then, when everyone had taken a tight grip of the sail, Jim's father gave the word, "Lift!"

With a hundred hands lifting together, they

soon carried the dolphin down to the sea where they laid him in the shallows and let the waves wash over him.

The dolphin squeaked and clicked and slapped the sea with his smiley mouth. He was swimming now, but he didn't seem to want to leave. He swam around and around.

"Off you go," Jim shouted, wading in and trying to push him out to sea. "Off you go." And off he went at last.

Everyone was clapping and cheering and waving goodbye. Jim just wanted him to come back again. But he didn't. Along with everyone else, Jim stayed and watched until he couldn't see him any more.

That day at school Jim could think of nothing but the dolphin. He even thought up a name for him. 'Smiler' seemed to suit him perfectly.

The moment school was over, Jim ran back to the beach hoping and praying Smiler might have come back. But Smiler wasn't there. He was nowhere to be seen.

Filled with sudden sadness he rushed down to

the pier. "Come back, Smiler!" he cried. "Please come back. Please!"

At that very moment, Smiler rose up out of the sea right in front of him! He turned over and over in the air before he crashed down into the water, splashing Jim from head to toe.

Jim didn't think twice. He dropped his bag, pulled off his shoes and dived off the pier.

At once Smiler was there beside him – swimming all around him, leaping over him, diving under him. Suddenly Jim found himself being lifted up from below. He was sitting on Smiler! He was riding him!

Off they sped out to sea, Jim clinging on as best he could. Whenever he fell off – and he often did – Smiler was always there, so that Jim could always get on again. The further they went, the faster they went. And the faster they went, the more Jim liked it.

Around and around the bay Smiler took him, and then back at last to the quay. By this time everyone in the village had seen them and the children were diving off the quay and swimming out to meet them.

All of them wanted to swim with Smiler, to touch him, to stroke him, to play with him. And Smiler was happy to let them. They were having the best time of their lives.

Every day after that, Smiler would be swimming near the quay waiting for Jim, to give him his ride. And every day the children swam with him and played with him too. They loved his kind eyes and smiling face.

Smiler was everyone's best friend.

Then one day, Smiler wasn't there. They waited for him. They looked for him. But he never came. The next day he wasn't there either, nor the next, nor the next.

Jim was broken-hearted, and so were all the children. Everyone in the village missed Smiler, young and old alike, and longed for him to come back. Each day they looked and each day he wasn't there.

When Jim's birthday came, his mother gave him something she hoped might cheer him up – a wonderful carving of a dolphin – she'd made it herself out of driftwood. But not even that seemed to make Jim happy.

Then his father had a bright idea. "Jim," he said, "why don't we all go out in the *Sally May*? Would you like that?"

"Yes!" Jim cried. "Then we could look for Smiler too."

So they hauled the *Sally May* down to the water and set the sails. Out of the bay they went, out on to the open sea where, despite her raggedy old sails, the *Sally May* flew along over the waves.

Jim loved the wind in his face, and the salt spray on his lips. There were lots of gulls and gannets, but no sight of Smiler anywhere. He called for him again and again, but he didn't come.

The sun was setting by now, the sea glowing gold around them.

"I think we'd better be getting back," Jim's father told him.

"Not yet," Jim cried. "He's out here somewhere. I know he is."

As the *Sally May* turned for home, Jim called

out one last time, "Come back, Smiler! Please come back. Please!"

Suddenly the sea began to boil and bubble around the boat, almost as if it was coming alive. And it WAS alive too, alive with dolphins! There seemed to be hundreds of them, leaping out of the sea alongside them, behind them, in front of them.

Then, one of them leapt clear over the *Sally May*, right above Jim's head. It was Smiler! Smiler had come back, and by the look of it he'd brought his whole family with him.

As the *Sally May* sailed into the bay everyone saw her coming, the dolphins dancing all about her in the golden sea. What a sight it was!

Within days the village was full of visitors, all of them there to see the famous dolphins and to see Smiler playing with Jim and the children.

And every morning, the *Sally May* and all the little fishing boats put to sea crammed with visitors, all of them only too happy to pay for their trip of a lifetime. They loved every minute of it, holding on to their hats and laughing with delight as the dolphins frisked and frolicked around them.

Jim had never been so happy in all his life. He had Smiler back, and now his father had all the money he needed to buy new sails for the *Sally May*. And all the other fishermen too could mend their sails and paint their boats. Once again, the village was a happy place.

As for the children...

... they could go swimming with the dolphins whenever they wanted to. They could stroke them, and swim with them and play with them, and even talk to them. But they all knew that only one dolphin would ever let anyone sit on him.

That was Smiler.

And they all knew that there was only one person in the whole world who Smiler would take for a ride.

And that was Jim.

THIS MORNING I MET A WHALE

This morning I met a whale. It was just after five o'clock and I was down by the river. Sometimes, when my alarm clock works, and when I feel like it, I get up early, because I like to go birdwatching, because birdwatching is my favourite hobby. I usually go just before first light. Mum doesn't mind, just so long as I don't wake her up, just so long as I'm back for breakfast.

It's the best time. You get to hear the dawn chorus. You get to see the sunrise and the whole world waking up around you. That's when the birds come flying down to the river to feed, and I can watch them landing in the water. I love that.

If you're already there when they come, they hardly notice you, and then you don't bother them. Hardly anyone else is down by the river at five o'clock, sometimes no one at all, just the birds and me. The rest of London is asleep. Well, mostly, anyway.

From our flat in Battersea it takes about five minutes to walk down to the river. The first bird I saw this morning was a heron. I love herons because they stand so still in the shallows. They're looking for fish, waiting to strike. When they strike they do it so fast, it's like lightning, and when they catch something they look so surprised and so pleased with themselves, as if they've never done it before. When they walk they will walk in slow motion. When they take off and fly they look prehistoric, like pterodactyls almost. Herons are my best. But soon enough they all came, all the other birds, the moorhens and coots, the crested grebes and the swans, the cormorants and the ducks. This morning I saw an egret too, perched on a buoy out in the river, and you don't see many of those. They're quite like herons, only much smaller, and white, snow-white. He was so beautiful. I couldn't take my eyes off him.

I was watching him through my binoculars, and he was looking right back at me. It was like he was asking me, "Hey, you, what are you doing here? This is my river, don't you know?" Suddenly, without any warning, he lifted off. Then they all lifted off, all the birds on the shore, all the birds in the river. It was really strange. It was just as if I'd fired a gun or something, but I hadn't. I looked around. There wasn't a single bird anywhere. They'd all disappeared. For a while the river was completely still and empty and silent, like it was holding its breath almost, waiting for something that was about to happen. I was doing the same.

Then I spotted something slicing slowly through the water towards me. It was a fin. *Shark!* I thought. *Shark!* And a warm shiver of fear crept up my back. Then I saw the head and knew at once it couldn't be a shark. It was more like a dolphin, but it wasn't. It wasn't quite the right shape. It was too big and too long to be a dolphin. It was big enough to be a whale, a real whale. Now I knew what it was. With a face like that I knew at once that it had to be a bottle-nosed whale. It's the only whale that's got a face like a dolphin. (I know quite a lot about whales because my uncle sent me a whale poster he'd got out of a newspaper, and I've had it pinned up in my bedroom over my bed ever since. So that's why I can recognise just about all the whales in the world – narwhals, belugas, sperm whales, pilot whales, minkies, bottle-nose whales, the lot.)

To begin with I just stood there and stared. I thought I was still dreaming. I couldn't take it in. I couldn't believe my eyes. I mean, a whale in the Thames, a whale in Battersea! He was close to the shore now, in shallower water, and still coming towards me. I could see almost all of him, from his head to his tail. But after a bit, I could see he wasn't really swimming any more, he was just lying there in the shallows, puffing and blowing a bit from time to time. *He must be resting*, I thought, *tired out after a long journey perhaps*. And then I noticed he was watching me as hard as I was watching him, almost like he was trying to stare me out, except I could tell from the gentleness in his eye that he wasn't being unfriendly towards me. He was interested in me, that's all, as interested as I was in him.

That's when I knew – don't ask me how, I just knew – that he wanted me to come closer to him. I climbed the wall and ran along the shore. The tide was already going out fast. I could see at once that he was in great danger. If he stayed where he was, he'd soon be stranded. I was walking slowly, so as not to alarm him. Then I crouched down as close as I could get to him, the water lapping all around me. His great domed head was only just out of my reach. We were practically face to face, eye to eye. He had eyes that seemed to be able to look right into me. He was seeing everything I was thinking.

I was sure he was expecting me to say something. So I did.

"What are you doing here?" I asked him. "You're a bottle-nose whale, aren't you? You shouldn't be here at all. You don't belong in the Thames. On my whale poster it says you live in the North Atlantic somewhere. So you should be up there, near Iceland, near Scotland maybe, but not down here. I've seen bottle-nose whales on the telly too, on *Planet Earth*, I think it was. There were lots of you all together. Or maybe it was pilot whales, I can't remember. But anyway, you always go around in schools, don't you, in huge family groups. I know you do. So how come you're all alone? Where's the rest of you? But maybe you're not all alone. Maybe some of your family came with you, and you got yourself a bit lost. Is that it?"

He kept staring back at me out of his big wide eye. I thought the best thing I could do was to just keep talking. I couldn't think what else to do. For a moment or two I didn't know what else to say, and anyway I suddenly felt a bit stupid talking to him. I mean, what if someone was watching me? Luckily, though, there was no one about. So instead, I looked upriver, back towards Battersea Bridge, to see if any of his family might have come with him, but everywhere the river was empty and glassy and still. There was nothing there, nothing that broke the surface anyway. He was alone. He'd come alone.

And that was when it happened. The whale spoke! I'm telling you the truth, honest. The whale spoke to me. His voice was like an echoing whisper inside my head, like a talking thought. But it was him talking. It really was, I promise you. "No," he said. "My family's not with me. I'm all on my own. They came some of the way with me, and they're waiting for me back out at sea. And you're right. We usually stay close to our families – it's safer that way. But I had to do this bit alone. Grandfather said it would be best. Grandfather would have come himself, but he couldn't. So I've come instead of him. Everyone said it was far too dangerous, that there was no point, that it's too late anyway, that people won't listen, that they just won't learn, no matter what. But Grandfather knew differently. He always said I should go, that time was running out, but there was still hope. I was young enough and strong enough to make the journey, he said. One of us had to come and tell you. So I came. There are some things that are so important that you just have to do them, whatever anyone says, however dangerous it might be. I believe that. And besides, I promised Grandfather before he died. I promised him I'd come and find you. And I always keep my promises. Do you keep your promises?"

I could just about manage a nod, but that was all. I tried, but I couldn't speak a word. I thought maybe I was going mad, seeing things that weren't there, hearing voices that weren't real, and suddenly that really terrified me. That was why I backed away from him. I was just about ready to run off when he spoke again.

"It's all right," he said. "Don't be frightened. I want you to stay. I want you to listen to me. I've come a very long way to talk to you, and I haven't got long."

His tail thrashed suddenly, showering me with water, and that made me laugh. But then I could see it was serious. He was rolling from one side to the other, rocking himself violently. Now I saw what it was that he was struggling to do. He was trying to back himself out into deeper water, struggling to keep himself afloat. I wanted to help him, but I didn't know how. All I could do was stand there and watch from the shore. It took him a while before he was out into deeper water and able to swim free again. He was blowing hard. I could tell he'd given himself a terrible fright. He swam off into the middle of the river, and then just disappeared completely under the water.

I stood there for ages and ages, looking for him up and down the river – he could have gone anywhere. I was longing for him to surface, longing to see him again, worried that he'd never dare risk it again. But he did, though when he came back towards me this time he kept his distance. Only his head was showing now, and just occasionally his fin. "I've got to watch it," he said. "The tide is going out all the time. Grandfather warned me about it, they all warned me. 'Stay clear of the shore,' they told me. 'Once you're beached, you're as good as dead.' We can breathe all right out of the water, that's not the problem. But we need water to float in. We can't survive long if we get stranded. We're big, you see, too heavy for our own good. We need water around us to survive. If we're not afloat we soon crush ourselves to death. And I don't want that to happen, do I?"

Maybe I got used to him speaking to me like this, I don't know. Or maybe I just wanted to hear more. Either way, I just didn't feel at all scared any more. I found myself walking back along the shore to be closer to him, and crouching down again to talk to him. I had things I needed to ask him.

"But I still don't really understand," I said. "You said you'd come to talk to me, didn't you? That means you didn't get lost at all, did you?"

"No, I didn't get lost," he told me. "Whales don't get lost, well not that often anyway. We tell each other where we are all the time, what's going on all around the world. What we see we share. So each and every one of us has a kind of map of the oceans, all the mountains and valleys under the sea, all the rivers and creeks, the coast of every continent, and every island, every rock

– it's inside our heads. We grow up learning it. That's why we don't get lost." He paused for a while, puffing hard through his blowhole. Talking was exhausting for him, I could see that.

"But we do get tired," he went on, "and we get old too, and we get sick, just like people do. We've a lot more in common with people than you know. We've got this earth in common for a start – and that's why I've come all this way to see you. We don't just share it with whales, but with every living thing. With people too. I've come to help you to save yourselves before it's too late, because if you save yourselves, then you'll be saving us too. It's like Grandfather said: we can't survive without you and you can't survive without us."

I didn't have a clue what he was on about, but I didn't dare say so. But I felt his eye searching out my thoughts. "You don't really know what I'm talking about, do you?" I shook my head. "Then I think the best thing I can do is to tell you about Grandfather, because it all began with Grandfather. When I was little, Grandfather was always going off on his travels, voyages of discovery, he called them. All over the world he went. We hardly ever saw him. Sometimes he was away for so long we all thought he was never coming back, and he wasn't all that good about keeping in touch either. He was a sort of adventurer, my grandfather, an explorer. He liked to go to places where no whale had ever been before.

"Then one day – it was some time ago now, when I was quite little – he came back from his travels and told us an amazing story. Ever since I first heard that story, I dreamed of going where Grandfather had gone, of seeing what he had seen. Grandfather had gone off to explore an unknown river, to follow it inland as far as he could go. No other whale had ever before dared to go there, as far as anyone knew anyway. All he knew of this river was that a couple of narwhals had been beached there in the mouth of the river a long time ago. They never made it back out to sea. The warning had gone out all over the oceans, and that was why whales had avoided the river ever since.

"It took a while for Grandfather to find it, but when he did he just kept on swimming. On and on he swam right into the middle of the biggest city he'd ever seen. It was teeming with life. Everywhere he looked there were great cranes leaning out over the river, and towering wharfs and busy docks. Everywhere there were boats and barges. He saw cars and trains and great red buses. And at night the lights were so bright that the whole sky was bright with them. It was a magical city, a place of bridges and towers and spires. And everywhere there were people, crowds of them, more than he'd ever seen before, more than he'd ever imagined there could be. He wanted to stay longer, to explore further upstream, to discover more. It was a wonderful place, but Grandfather knew it was dangerous too. The further upriver he swam, the shallower the waters around him were becoming. There were boats and barges everywhere, and he knew that if he wasn't very careful any one of them could run him down, and be the death of him. When a propeller took a nick out of his fin, he decided it was time to leave. And besides, he was weak with hunger. He knew he couldn't go any further.

"So he turned round and tried to swim back the way he'd come, back out to sea. But that was when he found that the tide was going down fast. He was having to keep to the deep channels, but so were all the boats and barges of course. There was danger all around him. He was so busy looking out for boats, that he didn't notice how shallow the water was getting all around him. Grandfather knew, as all whales do, just how easy it is to get yourself stranded. He always said it was his own fault. He lost concentration. But Grandfather got lucky. Some children saw him floundering there in the shallows, and came running down to the river to help him. They helped him back into the water, and then stayed with him till they were sure he was going to be all right. They saved his life, those children, and he never forgot it. 'When you get there, find a child,' he told me, 'because children are kind. They'll help you, they'll listen, they'll believe you.' So you see, it was only because of those children that Grandfather managed to find his way back out to the open sea again, and come back to us and tell us his story."

That was when I noticed that all the birds were back again, the egret too on his buoy out in the river. They had gathered nearby. There were pigeons and blackbirds perching on the trees behind me. On the shore not far away from me a beady-eyed heron stood stock still, and there was a family of ducks bobbing about on the river, a couple of cormorants amongst them, all looking at the whale but none of them too close. And like me, they were listening. Even the trees seemed to be listening.

The whale spoke again. "Grandfather told me exactly how to get here, just how many days south I had to swim. He said I had to look out for the fishing boats and their nets, not to hug the coastline, because that was where there were always more boats about. He warned me about the currents and the tides, told me where the deep channels were in the river, and not to show myself till I had to. I mustn't stay too long. I mustn't swim too far upriver. I mustn't go any further than I had to. 'You'll want to,' he told me, 'just like I did. When you find a child that'll be far enough. And when you find him, tell him all I've told you, what we whales all know and people refuse to understand. Tell him it's our last chance and their last chance. And you must make sure it's a child you tell. The old ones are greedy. They have hard hearts and closed minds, or they would not have done what they have done. They're too old to listen, too old to change. The young ones will listen and understand. Just like they saved me, they can save the world. If they know, they will want to put it right – I know they will. They just need telling. All you have to do is tell them.' That's what Grandfather told me. So that's why I have found you, and that's why I have come."

That was when I saw he was drifting closer and closer to the shore again. I was just about to warn him when he must have realised the danger himself, because suddenly his tail began to thrash wildly in the shallows. The birds took off in a great flurry of panic. The whale didn't stop flailing around till he'd found his way back out into deeper waters, where he dived down and vanished altogether. This time I wasn't really worried. I knew in my heart that he would come back, that he had much more to tell me. All the same, he was gone a long while before he appeared again, and I was so pleased to see him when at last he did.

It was the strangest thing, but when he began speaking to me again this time, I found I wasn't just hearing his words and understanding them. It was as if I could see in my mind everything he was telling me. I was seeing it all happen right there in front of my eyes. He wasn't just telling me. He was taking me round the world, round his world and showing me.

He showed me the bottom of the sea, where a coral reef lay dying and littered with rubbish. I saw a sperm whale being winched bleeding out of the sea, a leatherback turtle caught up in vast fishing nets, along with sharks and dolphins. There was an albatross too, hanging there limp and lifeless.

I saw the ice-cliffs in the Arctic falling away into the sea, and a polar bear roaming the ice, thin and hungry.

He showed me skies so full of smoke that day had become night, and below them the forests burning. An orang-utan was running for her life along a beach, clutching her infant, the hunters coming after her. I watched as they shot her down, and wrenched the screaming baby out of her arms. And then he showed me people, thousands upon thousands of them in a tented city by the sea, and a skeletal child lying alone and abandoned on the sand. She wasn't crying, because she was dead.

"Grandfather said all this killing has to stop. You are killing the sea we live in! You are killing the air we breathe. You are killing the world. Tell a child, Grandfather said. Only the children will put it right. That's why I came. That's why I found you. Will you put it right?"

"But how can I?" I cried.

"Tell them why I came. Tell them what I said.

Tell them they have to change the way they live. And don't just tell them. Show them. Will you do that?"

"Yes," I cried. "I promise!"

"But do you keep your promises?" he asked.

"I'll keep this one," I told him.

"That's all I needed to hear," he said. "Time for me to go now. I don't want to get myself beached, do I? I like your town. I like your river. But I'm more at home back in my sea."

"But what if you are beached?" I asked. "What if you die?"

"I'd rather not, of course," he said. "But like I told you, I had to come. It was important, the most important thing I ever did. I promised I'd do it, didn't I? Now I've done it. The rest is up to you."

And away he swam then, blowing loudly as he passed upriver under Battersea Bridge, so that the whole river echoed with the sound of it. There was a final flourish of his tail before he dived. It was like he was waving goodbye, so I waved back. I stayed there watching for a while just in case he came up again. All around me the birds were watching too. But that was the last we saw of him.

And that's the end of my story.

Mrs Fergusson was so delighted to see Michael writing away that she let him go on long after the others had finished. That's why she let him stay in all through breaktime too. She stayed in the classroom with him because she had some marking to do anyway. Every time she looked up Michael was still beavering away at his story. She'd never seen him so intent on anything, and certainly not on his writing. Until now, he'd always seemed to find writing rather difficult. She was intrigued. She was longing to ask him what he was writing about, but she didn't want to interrupt him.

Michael finished just as the bell went and everyone came rushing back into the classroom again, filling the place with noise. When they'd settled down Mrs Fergusson thought she'd try something she hadn't tried before with this class.

She asked if any of them would like to read their story out loud to the rest of the class. It was the last thing Michael wanted. They wouldn't believe him. They'd laugh at him, he knew they would. So he was very relieved when Elena, who always sat next to him, put up her hand. He was quite happy to sit there and listen to another of Elena's horsey stories. Elena was mad about horses. It was all she ever wrote about or talked about, all she ever painted too. Mrs Fergusson said it was good, but a bit short, and that perhaps it might be nice if she wrote about something else besides horses once in a while. Michael was looking out of the window, thinking of his whale deep down in the sea with his family all around him. So it caught him completely by surprise when she suddenly turned to him, and said, "Well, Michael, why don't you read us yours? What's it about?"

"A whale, miss," Michael replied.

She was coming over to his table. She was picking up his book. "A whale? That sounds really interesting," she said. "Goodness gracious. You've written pages and pages, Michael. You've never written this much before, have you? Would you like to read it for us?" Michael shook his head, which didn't surprise Mrs Fergusson at all. Michael was never one to volunteer himself for anything. "Your handwriting's a bit squiggly, but I think I can read it." She leafed through the pages. "Yes, I'm sure I can. Shall I read it out for you? You don't mind, do you, Michael?" Then she spoke to the whole class. "Would you like to hear Michael's whale story, children?" And they all did, so there was nothing Michael could do to stop her.

He had to sit there and listen like everyone else. He wanted to put his hands over his ears. He didn't dare to look up. He didn't want to have to see all those mocking smiles. To begin with, Mrs Fergusson read it like she always did, in her teachery voice, as if it was just a story. Then gradually, her whole tone seemed to change, and she was reading it as if she was inside the story and down by the river, as if she was seeing it all, hearing it all, feeling it all, as if she was longing to know what was going to happen. Michael dared to look around him now. No one was laughing. No one was even smiling. The longer the story went on, the more Mrs Fergusson's voice trembled, and the more silent the class became. When she'd finished she stood there for a long while, so moved she was unable to speak. But Michael was still waiting for the first sound of laughter, dreading it. Then, all of a sudden, Elena started clapping beside him, and moments later they were all clapping, including Mrs Fergusson who was smiling at him through her tears.

"An amazing story, Michael, the best I've read in a long, long time – and certainly the best you've ever written. Quite wonderful," she said. "Only one thing I would say, Michael," she went on. "It doesn't really matter of course, but if you remember, Michael, I did tell you it had to be a true story, about something that really happened."

"It is true, miss," Michael told her. "It all happened, just like I said. Honest."

That's when Jamie Bolshaw started sniggering and snorting. It spread all around the classroom until everyone was laughing out loud at him.

It didn't stop until Mrs Fergusson shouted at everyone to be quiet.

"You do understand what 'true' means, Michael, don't you?" she said. "It means not made up. If it is true, as you say it is, then that means that right now, just down the road, there's a bottle-nose whale swimming about in the river. And it means you actually met him, that he actually talked to you."

"Yes, miss. He did, miss," Michael said. "And I did meet him, this morning, early. Promise. About half past five, or six. And he did talk to me. I heard his voice and it was real. I wasn't making it up. But he's not there any more, miss, because he's gone back out to sea, like I said. It's true, all of it. I promise you, miss. It was just like I wrote it." And when Jamie Bolshaw started tittering again, Michael felt tears coming into his eyes. Try as he did, he couldn't hold them back, nor could he hold back the flood of words. He so wanted to make them believe him.

"It's true, miss, really true. When it was all over I ran back home. Mum was already having her breakfast. She told me I was late, that I'd better hurry or I'd be late for school. I told her why I was late. I told her all about the whale, the whole thing. She just said it was a good story, but that she didn't have time for stories just now, and would I please sit down and eat my breakfast. I said it was all true, every word of it. I crossed my heart and hoped to die. But she didn't believe me. So I gave up in the end and just ate my breakfast like she said.

"And when I got to school I didn't dare tell anyone, because I thought that if Mum didn't believe me, then no one else would. They'd just laugh at me, or call me a liar. I thought it would be best to keep quiet about it. And that's what I would have done. But you said we all had to write about something that had really happened to us. It could be funny or sad, exciting or frightening, whatever we wanted, you said, but it had to be true, really true. 'No fantasy, no science fiction, and none of your shock-horror stories, Jamie Bolshaw, none of that dripping blood stuff. I want you to write it down just as it happened, children, just as you remember it.' That's what you told us.

"And I couldn't think of anything else to write about except my whale. So that's what I wrote about. It was very long, the longest story and the most important story I've ever written. That's because I didn't want to leave anything out. I don't usually like writing stories, I'm no good at them. Can't get started, can't find a good ending. But this time it was like it was writing itself almost. All I had to do was to let it flow on to the page, down from my head, along my arm, through my fingers. Sometimes, though, it was really hard to concentrate, because I kept thinking about my whale, hoping and hoping he was out in the open sea by now, with his family again, safe again. The more I hoped it, the more I believed it, and the more I believed it the more I wanted to tell his story. That's why I stayed in all through breaktime to get it finished. It was raining anyway, so I didn't really mind."

When he'd finished there was a long silence.

"Yeah, yeah," Jamie sneered.

"That'll be quite enough of that, Jamie," Mrs Fergusson snapped, clapping her hands for silence. She could see now how upset Michael was becoming. "All right, Michael, all right. We'll say no more about it for the moment. Now children, what I want is for you to illustrate the story you've just written. Like that poem poster on the wall above the bookshelf – the tiger one, over there. I read it to you last week, remember? 'Tiger, tiger, burning bright'. I told you, didn't I? The poet illustrated it himself. And that's what I want you to do."

Through blinding tears Michael drew his bottle-nose whale, with the birds all around, the heron and the ducks and the cormorants, and the snowy white egret watching from the buoy. Then he drew himself, crouching down by the river's edge, with the sun coming up over London, all just as he'd seen it that morning. He had almost finished when, very surreptitiously, and making sure Mrs Fergusson wasn't looking, Elena slipped him a folded piece of paper. Michael opened it and read it. "Liar, liar, pants on fire." Elena was shaking her head and pointing at Jamie Bolshaw, who was making a face at him. That was the moment Michael lost it. He scrunched up the paper, walked across the classroom and hurled it at Jamie's grinning face. "I'm not a liar," he screamed at him. "I'm not, I'm not!"

Mrs Fergusson put Jamie in one corner and Michael in another. They hadn't been there five minutes before Mr Jenner, the head teacher, came in. Much to Michael's surprise and relief he didn't seem even to notice him standing there in the corner. He was pulling on his hat and coat. He was clearly going somewhere, and in an almighty hurry too. "Mrs Fergusson," he was saying. "I want your class to stop whatever it is that they're doing right now. I want them to get their coats on and assemble at once in the playground. And hurry, please."

"Why? What's going on?" Mrs Fergusson asked. "Is it a fire drill?"

"No, no, nothing like that. You're not going to believe this," Mr Jenner said, "but apparently there's a huge great whale in the river, right here, right now, just down the road from us. It's true. Not every day a whale comes to town, is it? It's on the telly. But we can see it for real. So I thought we'd all go and take a look. Quick as you can, please, else he could be gone before we get there, and we don't want that, do we?"

Everyone was gaping at Michael. For some time after Mr Jenner had left, no one said a word, not even Mrs Fergusson. But in spite of the look of utter amazement on Jamie Bolshaw's face, Michael could not for one moment enjoy his triumph. All he could think of was that his whale hadn't made it to the sea, that he must still be floundering in the river, still there, and trapped. He knew only too well what that might mean. He had to be there, now. He was out of the classroom, across the playground already full of excited children being herded into lines, and on his way down to the river before anyone could stop him.

By the time Michael arrived, there were crowds everywhere, hundreds of them lining the river on both sides, and all along Battersea

Bridge too. He pushed through the crowds and hoisted himself up on to the wall so he could see over. There were police down on the shoreline keeping everyone back behind the wall. From the moment he saw the whale Michael could see he was in serious trouble. He was wallowing helpless in the shallows, at the mercy of the tide, unwilling or unable to move.

Standing next to Michael was a building worker in a yellow hard hat and muddy boots. He was screaming down his mobile phone. "It's huge! Humungous, I'm telling you. Looks more like a bleeding shark to me. And he's going to get himself well and truly stuck in the mud if he's not careful, and that'll be his lot. Yeah, just below Battersea Bridge. I've got my yellow hat on, you can't miss me. I'll look out for you. No, he'll still be here. He's not going anywhere, poor blighter. And don't forget to bring the camcorder, right? This won't happen again. Once in a lifetime this."

There were half a dozen people around the whale, a couple of divers amongst them, trying to encourage him back into the water, but Michael could see it was no use. Without him the whale seemed to have lost all will to live. He was trying to decide what he could do, how he could get to the whale without being stopped by the police, when he found Mr Jenner beside him and Mrs Fergusson too, both breathless.

"You shouldn't have gone running off like that, Michael," said Mrs Fergusson. "You had us worried sick."

"He needs me," Michael told her. "I've got to go to him."

"You leave it to the experts," said Mr Jenner. "Come on over with the other children now. We've got a great view where we are."

"I don't want a great view," Michael shouted. "Don't you understand? I have to save him."

Michael didn't think twice after that. He climbed over the wall and raced along the shore towards the whale, dodging the police as he went. When Mr Jenner tried to call him back, Mrs Fergusson put her hand on his arm. "Best leave him be," she told him. "It's his whale. I'll go after him."

By the time the police managed to catch up with Michael, Mrs Fergusson was there to explain everything. They took some persuading, but in the end they said they could make an exception just this once, provided she stayed with him all the time, and provided both of them wore lifejackets, and didn't interfere.

So, along with several others, Michael and Mrs Fergusson were there when the tide began to rise, and at last the whale began to float free of the mud. Michael stayed as close to his head as he could get, and talked to him all the while to reassure him. "You'll be all right now," he said. "There's lots of us here, and we all want to help you. You'll swim out of here just like your grandfather did. All you have to do is swim. You must swim. You've got your whole family waiting for you out there. Do it for them. Do it for me."

They walked knee high with the whale out into the river, one of the divers swimming alongside him the whole time. Michael could see how hard the whale was trying. He was trying all he could, but he was so weak. Then, to the rapturous cheers of everyone around, the whale seemed suddenly to find strength enough to move his tail, and he managed to swim away from the shore, blowing hard as he went. They watched him turning slowly out in the middle of the river. And when everyone saw he was swimming the right way, another huge cheer went up. But Michael just wished they'd keep quiet. He sensed that all this noise must be bewildering and disorientating for him. But when the whale swam away under the bridge back towards the sea, even Michael joined in the cheering.

Like everyone else, when the whale dived down and disappeared, Michael thought he would be all right now, that he was well and truly on his way, that he'd make it this time for sure. But for some reason, by the time the whale surfaced again, he had turned and was coming back towards them. Within no time at all he had drifted back into the shallows, and despite all they tried to do to stop him, he had beached himself again.

Mrs Fergusson tried to stop him, so did the others, but Michael broke free of them and waded as far out into the river as he could, until he was as near to him as he could get. "You've got to swim!" he cried. "You've got to. Go under the bridge and just keep going. You can do it. Don't turn round. Don't come back. Please don't come back!"

There were people and boats everywhere, bustle and ballyhoo all around, so much of it that Michael could barely hear the whale when he spoke. "I'm trying," he said. "I'm trying so hard. But I'm very tired now, and I don't seem to know where I'm going any more. I'm feeling muddled in my head, and I'm so tired. I just want to sleep. I'm afraid that maybe I stayed too long. Grandfather warned me, they all warned me." His eyes closed. He seemed almost too exhausted to say anything more. Then his eyes opened again. "You do remember everything I said?" he whispered.

"Of course I do. I'll never forget. Never."

"Then it was worth it. No matter what happens,

it was worth it. Stay with me if you can. I need you with me."

So Michael did stay. He stayed all that day, and Mrs Fergusson stayed with him, long after all the other children had gone back home. By late afternoon his mother was there with them – they'd got a message to her at work. And the white egret stayed too, watching everything from his buoy.

As evening came on they tried to make Michael go home to sleep for a while.

"There's nothing more you can do here," his mother told him. "And anyway, you can watch it on the television. You can't stay here all night. You'll catch your death. We'll get a pizza on the way. What do you say?" Michael stayed crouching down where he was. He wasn't moving.

"I tell you what, Michael," Mrs Fergusson said, "I'll stay. You go home and get some rest, and then you can come back in the morning. I won't leave him, honestly I won't. And I'll phone if anything happens. How's that?"

Between them they managed to persuade him.

Michael knew everything they said was true. He was tired, and he was cold, and he was hungry. So in the end he agreed, just so long as he could come back in the morning, at first light, he said.

"I won't be long," he whispered to the whale. "I'll be back soon, I promise."

Back at home in a hot bath he shivered the cold out of him, but all the while he was thinking only of his whale.

He ate his pizza watching his whale on the television. He knew he couldn't go to bed. He didn't want to sleep. He wanted only one thing, to be back down by the riverside with his whale. He begged his mother again and again to let him go, but she wouldn't let him. He had to get some sleep, she said.

There was only one thing for it. He would wait till his mother had gone to bed, then he'd get dressed and slip out of the flat. That's what he did. He ran all the way back down to the river.

All the rescue team and the divers were still there, and so was Mrs Fergusson, sitting by the wall wrapped in a blanket. And everywhere there were still dozens of onlookers. The egret was there on his buoy. And the whale was floundering near the shore, not far from where Michael had left him. But there was something else out on the river. It looked like a barge of some kind, and it hadn't been there before – Michael was sure of it. He ran over to Mrs Fergusson.

"Miss, what's that barge there for?" he asked her. "What's going on?"

"They're going to lift him, Michael," she said. "They had a meeting, and they decided it's the only way they can save him. They don't think he can do it on his own, he's too weak and disorientated. So they're going to lift him on to that barge and carry him out to sea."

"They can't!" Michael cried. "They'll kill him if they do. He can't live out of the water, he told me so. He's my whale. I found him. They can't, they mustn't! I won't let them!"

Michael didn't hesitate. He dashed down to the shore and waded out into the river. When he found he couldn't wade any more, he began to swim. A few short strokes and he was alongside the whale. He could hear Mrs Fergusson and the others shouting at him to come back. He paid them no attention. The whale looked at him out of his deep dark eye.

"I need you with me," he whispered.

"I know. I'm back," Michael said. "Are you listening? Can you hear me?"

"I hear you," replied the whale.

"I'm going to swim with you," Michael told him. "I'm a really good swimmer. We're going together. You just have to follow me. Can you do that?"

"I'll try," said the whale.

From the bank they all saw it, Michael and the whale swimming away side by side towards Battersea Bridge. They could hardly believe their eyes. They could see the whale was finding it hard, puffing and blowing as he went, that Michael was battling against the tide. But incredibly, they were both making some headway. By now the rescue team had sent out an inflatable to fetch Michael in. Everyone could see what was bound to happen in the end, that the tide was against them, that it was too cold, that it was impossible. Both the boy and the whale tired together. They hauled Michael out of the water, and brought him back to the shore. From there he had to watch his whale swim bravely on for a few more minutes, before he had to give up the unequal struggle. Even Michael knew now that there was nothing more he could do, that the barge was the whale's only chance of survival.

Michael was there on the shore with his mother and Mrs Fergusson later that morning when they hoisted the whale slowly from the water, and swung him out in a great sling on to the barge that would take him off to sea. With the world watching on television, followed by a procession of small boats, the barge carried him along the river, under the bridges, past Westminster and the London Eye and St Paul's, out towards Greenwich and the Thames Barrier and to the sea beyond. There was a vet on hand to monitor his progress all the way. And Michael too never left the whale's side, not for one moment. He stayed by him, pouring water over him from time to time, to keep his skin moist, soothing him and talking to him to reassure him, to keep his spirits up, all the while hoping against hope that the whale would have the strength to survive long enough to reach the open sea.

Michael didn't have to ask, he could see the vet was not optimistic. He could see his whale was failing fast. His eyes were closed now, and he had settled into a deep sleep. He was breathing, but only barely. Michael thought he did hear him breathe just one more word.

"Promise?" he said.

"I promise," Michael replied. He knew exactly what he was promising, that he would spend his whole life keeping it. And then the whale simply stopped breathing. Michael felt suddenly very alone.

The vet was examining him. After a while he looked up, wiping the tears from his face. "Why?" he asked. "I don't understand. Why did he come? That's what I'd like to know."

Ahead of them, as they came back into the

heart of London, flew a single white bird. It was the snowy egret that had never left the whole way out and the whole way back. All London seemed still with sadness as they passed by under Tower Bridge.

On 20 January 2006, an eighteen-foot (five-metre) northern bottle-nosed whale was spotted swimming up the Thames past the Houses of Parliament. She swam up as far as Battersea Bridge where she became stranded. For two days rescuers battled to save the whale, as the world looked on, hoping for the best. But in spite of everyone's efforts that whale died before the rescue pontoon on which she was being transported could reach the safety of the open sea.

Meet another special animal in Sarah Lean's
story about a brave little dog called Jack Pepper.

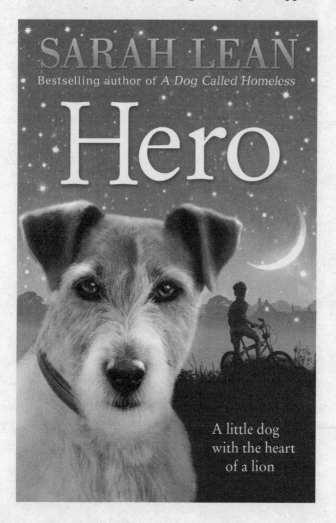

SARAH LEAN

Bestselling author of *A Dog Called Homeless*

Hero

A little dog
with the heart
of a lion

Turn the page to read an extract.

1.

I can fit a whole Roman amphitheatre in my imagination, and still have loads of room. It's big in there. Much bigger than you think. I can build a dream, a brilliant dream of anything, and be any hero I want…

For most awesome heroic imagined gladiator battles ever, once again the school is proud to present the daydreaming trophy to… Leo Biggs!

That's also imaginary. You have to pass your trumpet exam to get a certificate (like my big sister Kirsty), or be able to read really fast and remember tons of facts to get an A at school (like my best mate George), before anyone tells you that they're proud of you. Your family don't even get you a new bike for your birthday for being a daydreamer, even if you really wanted one.

Daydreaming is the only thing I'm good at and, right here in Clarendon Road, I am a gladiator. The best kind of hero there is.

"Don't you need your helmet?" George called.

"Oh, yeah, I forgot," I said, cycling back on my old bike to collect it. "Now stand back so you're in the audience. Stamp your feet a bit and do the thumbs-up thing at the end when I win."

George sat on Mrs Pardoe's wall, kicking against the bricks, reading his book on space.

"It says in here that meteors don't normally hit the earth," George said, "they break up in the atmosphere. So there aren't going to be any explosions or anything when it comes. Shame."

"Concentrate, George. You have to pretend you're in the amphitheatre; they didn't have books in Roman times… did they?"

"Uh, I don't think so. They might have had meteors though. People think you can wish on meteors, but it's not scientific or anything."

He didn't close the book and I could tell he was still concentrating on finding out more about the meteor that was on the news. So I put on my gladiator helmet (made out of cardboard, by me) and bowed to my imaginary audience. They rumbled and cheered.

"Jupiter's coming now. Salute, George, salute!"

The king of all the Roman gods with arms of steel and a chest like hills, rolled into the night stars over Clarendon Road like a tsunami. Jupiter was huge and impressive. He sat at the back of the amphitheatre on his own kind of platform and throne, draped his arm over the statue of his lion and nodded. It was me he'd come to watch.

I held up my imaginary sword.

"George!"

George punched the sky without looking up from his book. He couldn't see or hear what I could: the whole crowd cheering my name from the thick black dark above.

Let the games begin! Jupiter boomed.

The gate opened.

"Here he comes, George!"

"Get him, Leo, get him good."

The gladiator of Rome came charging up the slope. I twisted and turned on my bike, bumped down off the kerb and picked up speed. *The crowd were on their feet already and I raised my sword…*

And then George's mum came round the corner.

"George! You're to come in now for your tea," she said.

I took off my helmet and put it inside my coat.

"In a minute!" George said. "I'm busy."

"It's freezing out here," she said.

I skidded over on my bike. I whispered, "George! Please stay! It is my birthday. You have to be here, I have to win something today."

"I'm fine," he called to his mum. "I've got a hat."

"Yes, but you're not wearing it." She came over, pressed her hand to George's forehead. "You've got homework and you're definitely running a temperature."

"Gladiators don't have homework," I said. George grinned.

"But George does," his mum said.

"Mum!" His shoulders sagged.

She shook her head. "I think you both

ought to be inside. Come on, George, home now."

"Sorry, gotta go," he sighed. He slipped off the wall, pulled at the damp from the frosty wall on the back of his trousers. "I'll come and watch tomorrow."

"Do your coat up," George's mum said as they walked away.

George turned back. "Did you know that Jupiter is just about the closest it ever gets to earth right now?"

I looked up. Jupiter was here, in the night sky over Clarendon Road.

"Yeah, I know, George."

"I'll do some research for our Roman presentation."

"Yeah, good one, see you tomorrow."

"Leo!"

"What?"

He saluted.

I didn't want to go home yet though. I really wanted something to go right today.

I bumped the kerb on my bike, cruised back into the arena.

The gladiator of Rome was lurking in the shadows between the parked cars. I could smell his sweaty fighting smell, heard his raspy breath. Just in time I hoisted my sword over my head as he attacked. Steel clashed. I held his weight, heaved, turned, advanced, swung. We smashed our swords together again. I felt his strength and mine.

The crowd were up: thousands of creatures and men stamped their feet in the amphitheatre of the sky. Their voices roared. Swords locked, I ducked, twisted, to spin his weapon from his hands. I didn't see the fallen metal dustbin on the pavement. I braked but my front wheel thumped into the side of it. I catapulted over the bin and landed on the pavement.

The crowd groaned. Jupiter held out his arm, his fist clenched. He punched his thumb to the ground.

I'd never thought that I could lose in my own imagination. Maybe I wasn't even that good at imagining. I lay there, closed my eyes, sighed. It warmed the inside of my cardboard helmet but nothing else. Everything was going wrong today.

I opened my eyes but it wasn't the gladiator of Rome looking down at me. It was a little white dog.

2.

I DIDN'T KNOW IF DOGS HAD IMAGINATIONS or if they thought like us at all, but this little dog looked me right in the eye and turned his head to the side as if he was asking the same question that I was: *How can you lose when you're the hero of your own story?* Which was a bit strange seeing as nobody can see what's in your imagination.

I leaned up on my elbows and stared back. The dog had ginger fur over his ears and eyes, like his own kind of helmet hiding who he really was, and circles like ginger biscuits on his white back.

"Did you see the size of that gladiator?" I said.

The little dog looked kind of interested, so I said, "Do you want to be a gladiator too?"

I think he would have said yes, but just then a great shadow loomed over us.

"Is that you dreaming again, Leo Biggs?" a voice growled.

It was old Grizzly Allen. He had one of those deep voices like it came from underground. If you try and talk as deep as him it hurts your throat.

Grizzly is our neighbour and the most loyal customer at my dad's cafe just round the corner on Great Western Road – Ben's Place. Grizzly was always in there. It was easier and a lot better than cooking for one, he said.

You might tell a dog what you're imagining, or your best mate, but you don't tell everyone because it might make you sound stupid.

"I didn't see the bin. I couldn't stop."

Grizzly held out his hand and pulled me up like I was a flea, or something that weighed nothing.

"No bones broken, eh?" he beamed. "Perhaps just something bruised."

I checked over my bike. The chain had come off and the rusted back brake cable was frayed.

"Aw, man!" I sighed.

"Bit small for you now," Grizzly said. "Can't be easy to ride."

"Yeah, I know. I need a new one." I shrugged,

but I didn't really want to talk about that. I'd had this bike for four years, got it on my seventh birthday; the handlebars had worn in my grip. They were smooth now, like the tyres and the brake pads and the saddle. I didn't want to say anything about how I'd thought my parents were getting me a new one for my birthday, today. I guessed they didn't think I deserved it yet. It wasn't like I'd passed my Grade 6 trumpet exam, like Kirsty had.

Grizzly picked up my bike as if it was as light as a can-opener, leaned it against his wall and lowered himself down, all six feet four of him folded into a crouch.

"Can't do anything with this here cable." He sort of growled in his throat, but I didn't know if that was because he couldn't fix it or because he was uncomfortable hunkered down like that.

The little dog watched Grizzly's hairy hands feeding the chain back on the cogs. Grizzly didn't have a dog and it looked odd, a great big man with that little white and ginger dog standing, all four legs square, by his side.

"Did you get a new dog, Grizzly?"

Actually there was nothing new about that dog, except he was new here in our road. I don't mean he looked old, because he didn't. He was almost buzzing with life. There was something ancient about him though. Like one of the gold Roman coins in our museum. Sort of shiny and fresh on the outside, but with years and years of history worn into them.

"He's not mine," Grizzly said. "This here is Jack Pepper." The little dog watched Grizzly's broad face and his tail swayed at the sound of his own name.

WORLD BOOK DAY *fest*

WORLD BOOK DAY · 5 MARCH 2015

A BIG, HAPPY, BOOKY CELEBRATION OF READING

≫ Want to READ more? ≪

VISIT your local bookshop

- Get some great recommendations for what to read next
- Meet your favourite authors & illustrators at brilliant events
- Discover books you never even knew existed!

FIND YOUR LOCAL BOOKSHOP — www.booksellers.org.uk/bookshopsearch

JOIN your local library

You can browse and borrow from a HUGE selection of books and get recommendations of what to read next from expert librarians—all for **FREE**! You can also discover libraries' wonderful children's and family reading activities.

FIND YOUR LOCAL LIBRARY — www.findalibrary.co.uk

Get ONLINE!

Visit WORLDBOOKDAY.COM to discover a whole new world of books!

- Downloads and activities for **FAB** books and authors
- Cool games, trailers and videos
- Author events in your area
- News, competitions and new books —all in a **FREE** monthly email

and MORE!

Win an iPad Mini
and four stunning e-books

If you enjoyed *Best Mates*, then discover more incredible stories from master-storyteller

michael morpurgo

To enter, visit www.michaelmorpurgo.com/competition
Submit the correct answer to the question and the winner will
be picked at random from all correct entries we receive.

www.michaelmorpurgo.com

...rCollins *Children's Books*